Tiny Teddy

Tidies Up

Tiny Teddy
Tidies Up

Lucy Byng

BAREFOOT BEGINNERS

Tiny Teddy likes to
tidy up.

Every day he has
a job to do.

On busy days,
Tiny Teddy goes to
the bottle bank.

Bang, clatter, crash!
He likes to hear
the bottles smash.

On quiet days,
Tiny Teddy checks
his compost.

Sniff, sniff!
The smells make his
nose twitch.

On windy days,
Tiny Teddy does
his washing.

This is fun!
His clothes dry
quickly in the sun.

On chilly days,
Tiny Teddy cleans
his loo.

Splash, splish!
He likes to watch the
vinegar swish.

On snowy days,
Tiny Teddy feeds
the birds.

Shake, shake!
The birds enjoy a
morning break.

On rainy days,
Tiny Teddy writes
and draws.

Only use scrap paper,
please! Saving paper
saves the trees.

On sunny days,
Tiny Teddy tends
his roses.

Here's a treat!
Tea leaves make roses
strong and sweet.

On lazy days,
Tiny Teddy paints
and plays.

These are teddy's
favourite days.

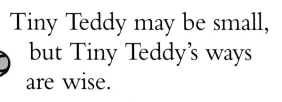

Tiny Teddy may be small, but Tiny Teddy's ways are wise.

You can write to Tiny Teddy about the things you do in your home. This is his address:

Tiny Teddy
PO Box 95
Kingswood
Bristol BS15 5RW

BAREFOOT BOOKS Ltd
PO Box 95
Kingswood
Bristol BS15 5RW

This book has been printed on 100% acid-free paper
illustrations © 1994 by Lucy Byng

First published in Great Britain in 1994 by Barefoot Books Ltd
Printed and bound by Lego, Vicenza, Italy
ISBN: 1 898000 96 4